Mel Bay's Master Accordion Scale Book
With Jazz Scale Studies

By
Gary Dahl

1 2 3 4 5 6 7 8 9 0

Visit us on the Web at www.melbay.com — E-mail us at email@melbay.com

Table of Contents

Foreword

Why do we practice scales? The great jazz accordionist, Art Van Damme, when asked what he practiced replied, "Only the fundamentals!" This book will attempt to present "those fundamentals" in a practical concise presentation.

The music came first and then the theory. Scale Theory can be a very complicated and intensive subject because of the many possible variations. While studying privately and at the university level I encountered numerous overly-complicated texts. Instead this book will utilize the practical, real world tools that will enhance professional musicianship. At first it is important to master all of the twelve major scales so they become a reflex. This book will also present the primary scales for jazz and modal theory.

Use this book with or before *The Chord Melody Method for Accordion and Keyboards*, MB97343BCD.

Gary Dahl

This book is dedicated to Art Van Damme;
the original jazz accordionist that inspired
the author from the beginning to the present.

About the Author

Gary Dahl is widely known as a virtuoso accordionist as well as a composer, arranger, recording artist and music educator, with an extensive background in music theory, composition and harmony. Gary has now developed an impressive body of work including hundreds of individual arrangements and more than a dozen books currently in publication by Mel Bay Publications.

As a recognized teacher, Gary provides specialized training for all levels of students. Gary's students have won national and state competitions as well as achieving professional status. While Gary resides in Puyallup, Washington near Seattle he provides lessons by correspondence for students worldwide. www.accordions.com/garydahl

Gary currently performs as a single for private functions. The Gary Dahl trio plus vocalist performed regularly at private clubs, hotels and the lounge circuit from 1960 through 1991. Gary is a graduate of the University of Washington specializing in composition and theory and is a former commercial corporate pilot, flight instructor and corporate sales manager.

Lets Get Started!

Practice all scales STACCATO & LEGATO (Same as slurring, smoothly connected)

Staccato: "Tap" the keys quickly and lightly | fingers & wrist only; similar to bouncing a basketball | do not use the arm; stay relaxed.

Legato: Lift each finger and strike each key | similar to a hammer hitting a nail.

C Major

Repeat 20 times before the next section without pausing. Repeat 10 times or more.
Start slowly & gradually increase speed. Keep it even. Use this procedure for each scale.

G Major

The passing under with the thumb and crossing over with the 3rd or 4th finger is a little more difficult on a vertical keyboard. **Make sure your accordion is correctly positioned.**

Stretching & bending... do this exercise between each scale practice to exaggerate the process for flexibility and control.

Legato only

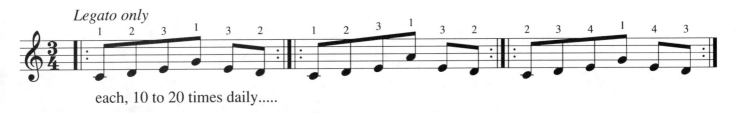

each, 10 to 20 times daily.....

Accordion positioning: The right strap should be longer than the left strap. The left strap is tight and determines the proper height. The top of the treble keyboard should be as high as possible (2 -3 inches below the chin).The black keys should be under the chin and vertical with the center line of the upper body.
Do not position the treble keyboard inside the right thigh. Keep knees as low as possible.

D Major

Hint: Start with belows closed and maintain steady medium pressure.

A Major

Hint: Occasionally sing all scales presented in this book.

E Major

B Major

*Make sure 4th finger is close to the black keys but not inside the black keys.

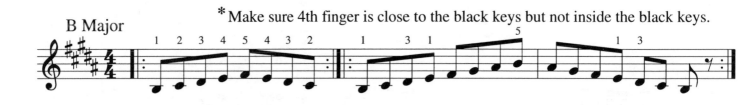

F♯ Major or G♭ Major *

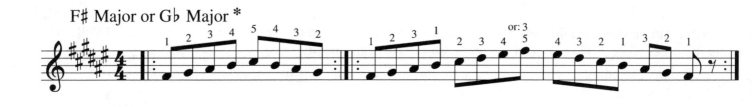

C♯ Major or D♭ Major 5 Flats

(C♯ Major, 7 Sharps)   (F♯ Major, 6 Sharps)
D♭ Major, 5 Flats   G♭ Major, 6 Flats

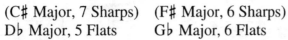

F Major

B♭ Major

E♭ Major

A♭ Major

D♭ Major

G♭ Major

7

Exercises for the right hand only.
Major & Minor Scales

Practice one scale at a time. Play slowly
at first then fast and even.

Melodic Minor: 6th & 7th raised ascending and
the **Natural Minor** descending. (Key Signature)

Review directions at the top of page 1

C Major Scale
Allegro

Relative minor key is the
6th of the relative major scale.

C Major Scale in 3rds

A Minor - Melodic

Same as A Major Ascending

Relative major is the
3rd of the minor scale.

Natural Minor Descending

3rds

A Minor - Harmonic

Harmonic Minor: 7th degree
is raised; ascending and descending.

Relative major is the
3rd of the minor scale.

3rds

Chromatic Scale in 3rds

*Note: Fingering for 3rds vary from player to player. Decide the best for each situation.

G Major Scale

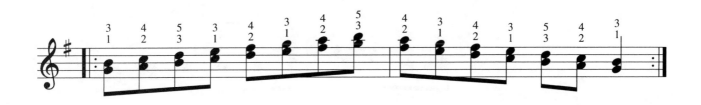

E Minor - Melodic

E Minor - Harmonic

D Major Scale

B Minor - Melodic

B Minor - Harmonic

A Major Scale

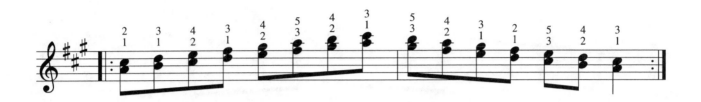

F♯ Minor - Melodic

F♯ Minor - Harmonic

E Major Scale

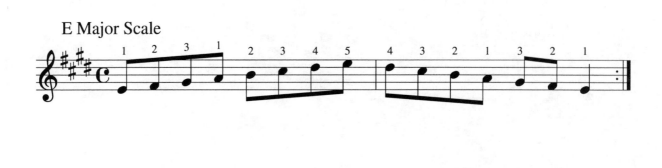

C# Minor - Melodic

C# Minor - Harmonic

B Major Scale

G♯ Minor - Melodic

G♯ Minor - Harmonic

F♯ Major Scale

D♯ Minor - Melodic

D♯ Minor - Harmonic

13

C# Major Scale

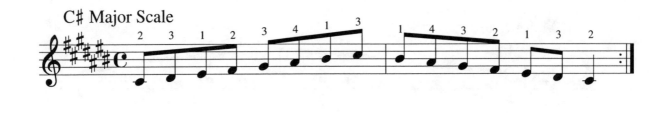

A# Minor - Melodic

A# Minor - Harmonic

F Major Scale

D Minor - Melodic

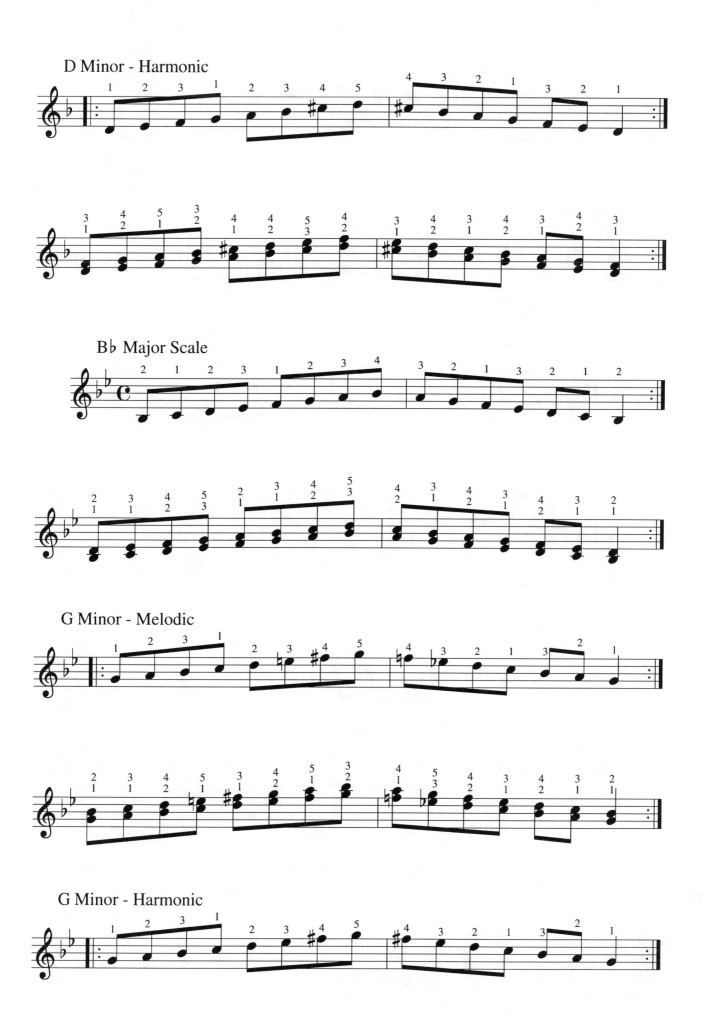

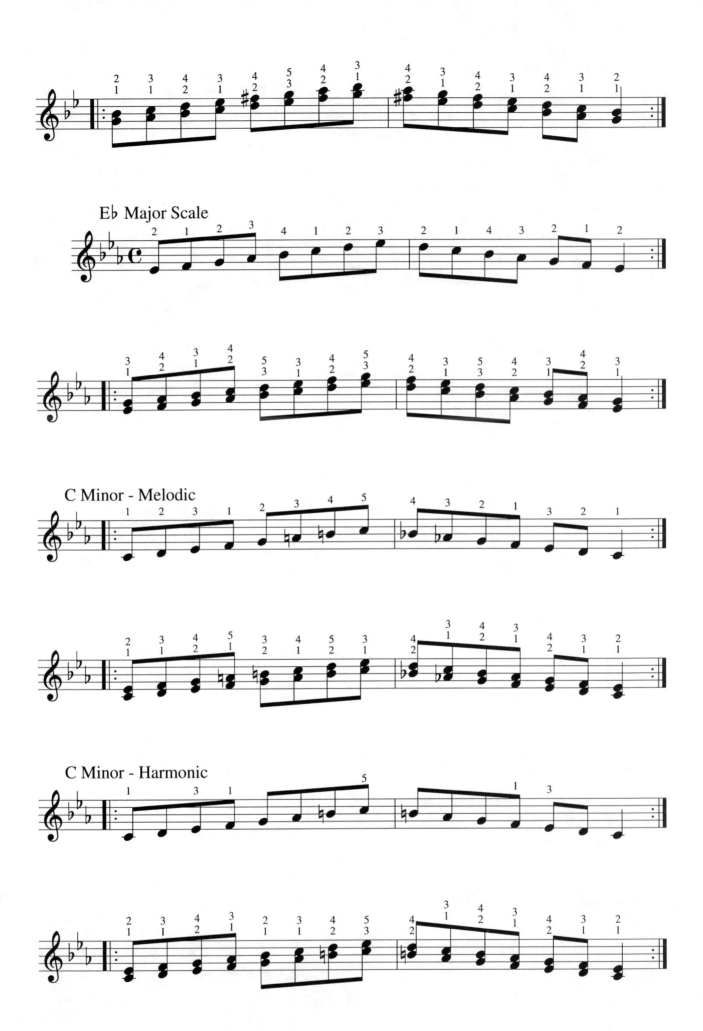

Eb Major Scale

C Minor - Melodic

C Minor - Harmonic

NOTE: Melodic minor descending is the natural minor and is also known as the aeolian mode. The natural minor uses the exact key signature.

Ab Major Scale

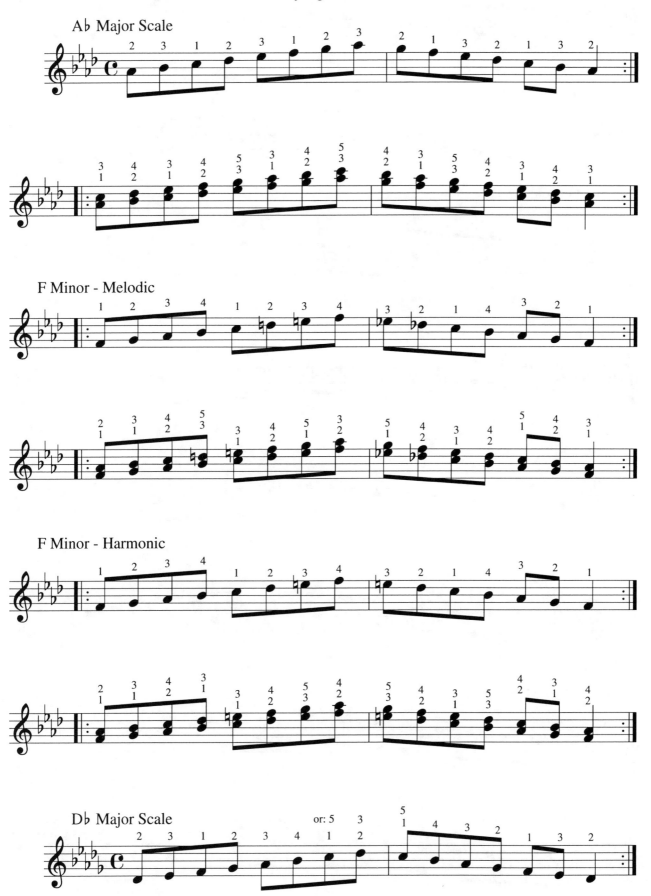

F Minor - Melodic

F Minor - Harmonic

Db Major Scale

The 12 Major Scales in 2 Octaves

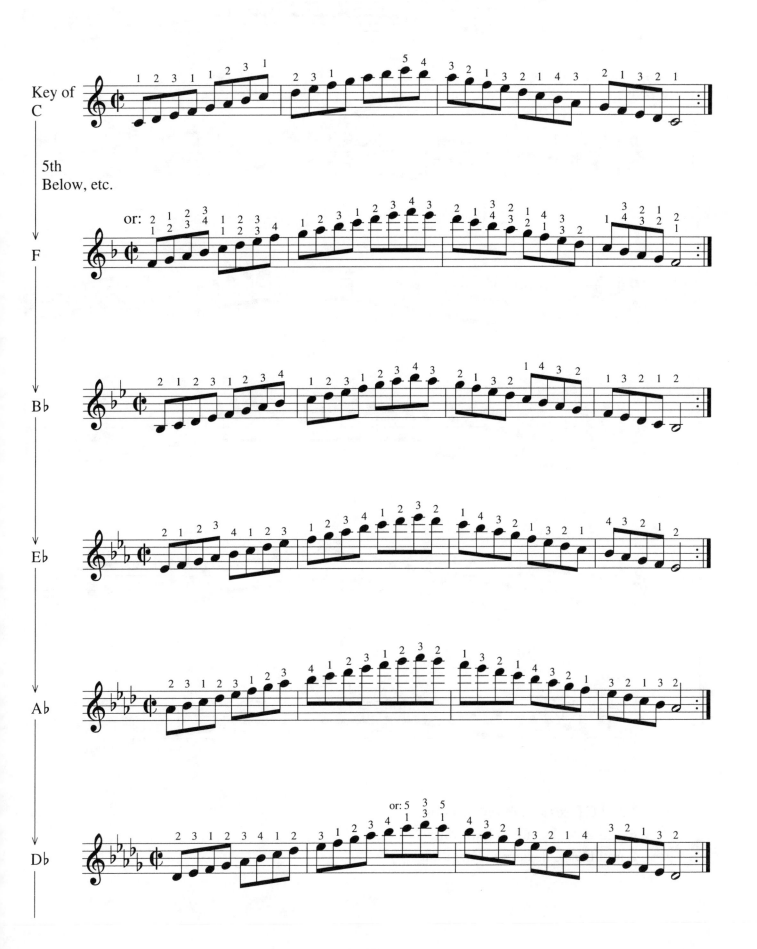

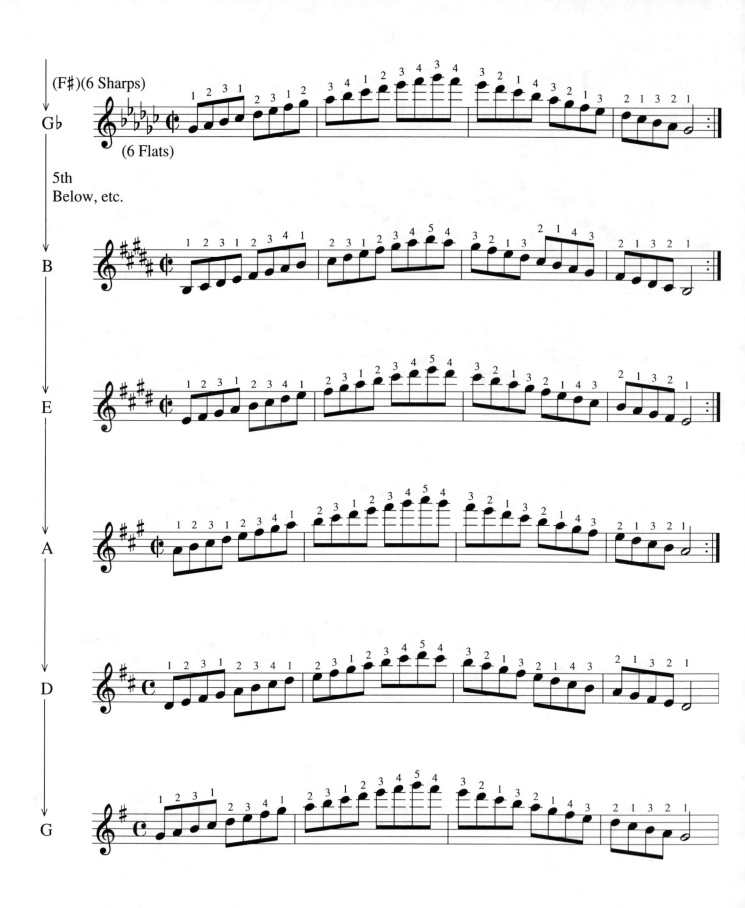

F♯ and G♯ scales are enharmonic
C♭ and B scales are enharmonic
C♯ and D♭ scales are enharmonic

All Major scales in the left hand use identical fingering and sequence.

C Major

Repeat until a natural reflex.

Hint: Do not make any errors and or wrong directional moves while practicing ... this philosophy is the same for both hands. Remember to practice slowly to be error free.

Practice All Major Scales in unison and contrary motion.

Unison Example

C Major

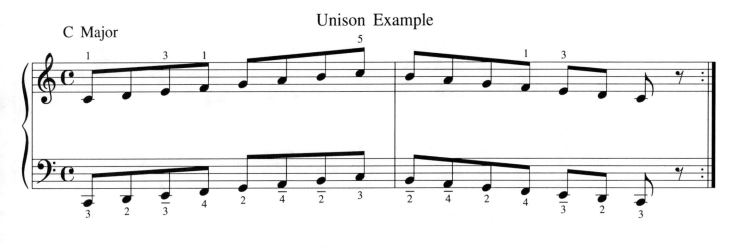

Contrary Motion Example

C Major

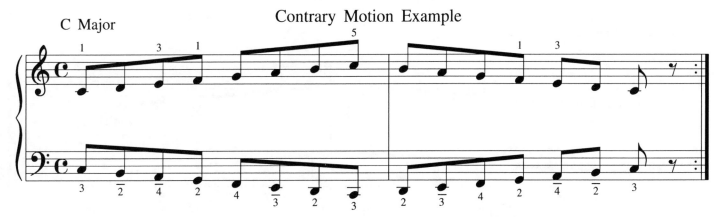

Hint: Memorize all major scales in one octave and two octaves. Remember, all L. H. major scales use identical fingering and will not require any written out charts.

Chromatic fingering for the accordion is a little different than piano descending because of the vertical keyboard.

Ascending

Hint: Drop the wrist a little lower than fingertips.

(Note the use of the 2nd finger)

Descending

Descending:

Hint: Wrist will be a little higher (toward chin) than the fingertips. There are, of course variations in fingering to suit the music. (Starting and ending locations) 4th & 5th fingers are occasionally used.

Practice using 3rds... all keys

6ths... Practice in all keys

Chromatic Scale L. H.

L. H. Harmonic Minor... Memorize, and practice in all keys.
(Note: Play counterbass only when the dash is under the fingering.)

best: $\frac{4}{3}$ $\frac{2}{2}$ $\frac{3}{5}$ $\frac{2}{3}$ $\frac{4}{2}$ 5 2 3 2 5 $\frac{4}{2}$ $\frac{2}{3}$ $\frac{3}{5}$ $\frac{2}{4}$ $\frac{4}{2}$
or: 3

(There are other optional fingerings... the author feels this is the best for minimal stretching)

A Melodic Minor

$\overline{4}$ $\overline{2}$ 3 2 $\overline{4}$ $\overline{3}$ $\overline{2}$ 3 4 5 $\overline{4}$ 2 4 $\overline{3}$ 2

(Review)
Theory:

A Minor & C Major scales share the same key signature and are relative.

(Review) See pg. 4

The Harmonic Minor scale raises the 7th degree of the scale 1/2 step.

(Review) See pg. 4

The Melodic Minor scale raises the 6th & 7th degrees 1/2 step ascending and returns to the natural minor descending.

Example: The A natural Minor scale

5
1   3   1   1   3

Theory cont'd

C Melodic Minor Descending

(Return to Natural Minor Scale)
(same as the key signature)

Key signature of C minor

C AEOLIAN
♭7, ♭6 and ♭3 when ascending and
descending and disregarding
the key signature

Practice all ascending melodic minor scales

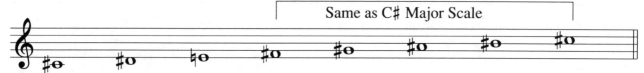

The descending melodic minor scale is not used and or not suggested for jazz improvisation.

C Melodic Minor

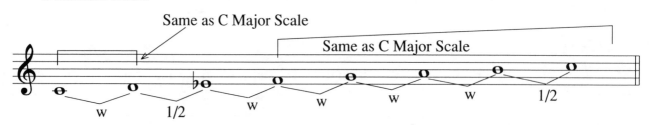

D♭ Melodic Minor (Enharmonic to C♯)

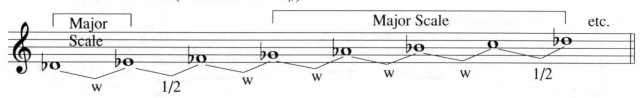

24

Practice

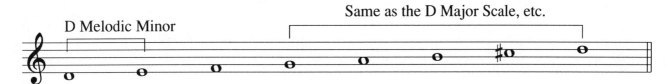

D Melodic Minor — Same as the D Major Scale, etc.

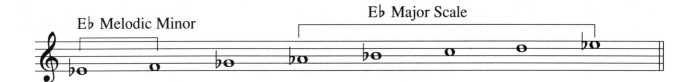

E♭ Melodic Minor — E♭ Major Scale

E Melodic Minor — E Major Scale

F Melodic Minor — F Major Scale

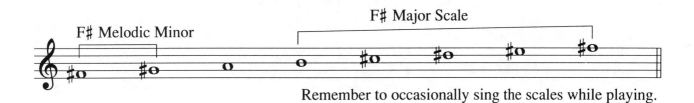

F♯ Melodic Minor — F♯ Major Scale

Remember to occasionally sing the scales while playing.

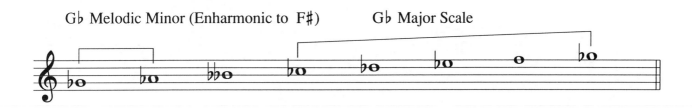

G♭ Melodic Minor (Enharmonic to F♯) — G♭ Major Scale

G Melodic Minor   **G Major Scale**

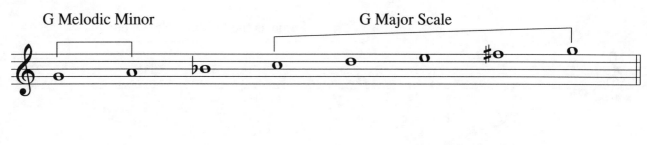

A♭ Melodic Minor   **A♭ Major Scale**

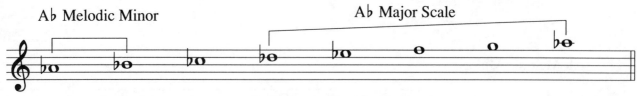

A Melodic Minor   **A Major Scale**

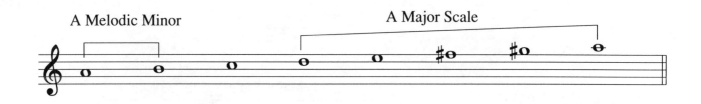

B♭ Melodic Minor   **B♭ Major Scale**

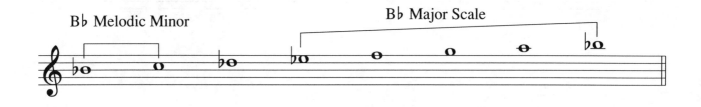

B Melodic Minor   **B Major Scale**

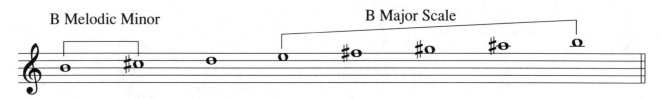

Again, practice and review to play as a reflex. (on automatic)

The Diminished Scale

(Also known as the symmetrical scale)

Symmetrical scales (Diminished Scales) are those having regular recurring intervals. Other scales we have studied previously in this book all include 2 or 3 half steps which occur at certain points on the scales. Symmetrical scales can be composed entirely of whole steps or half steps or an equal number of certain intervals. Also, this group of scales relates to chords which have altered chord tones.

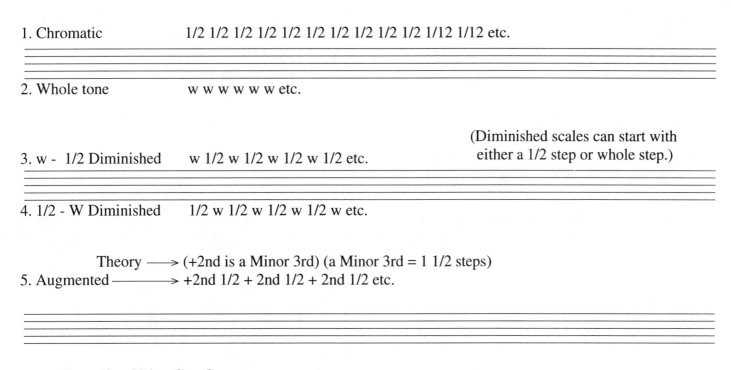

1. Chromatic   1/2 1/2 1/2 1/2 1/2 1/2 1/2 1/2 1/2 1/2 1/12 1/12 etc.

2. Whole tone   w w w w w w etc.

(Diminished scales can start with either a 1/2 step or whole step.)

3. w - 1/2 Diminished   w 1/2 w 1/2 w 1/2 w 1/2 etc.

4. 1/2 - W Diminished   1/2 w 1/2 w 1/2 w 1/2 w etc.

Theory ⟶ (+2nd is a Minor 3rd) (a Minor 3rd = 1 1/2 steps)

5. Augmented ⟶ +2nd 1/2 + 2nd 1/2 + 2nd 1/2 etc.

Examples: Using C to C

Chromatic Scale

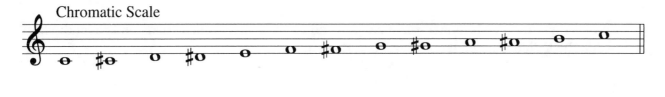

Whole tone scale   (6 tone scale)   (6 whole steps)
(omits one letter)   (only 2 different whole tone scales)

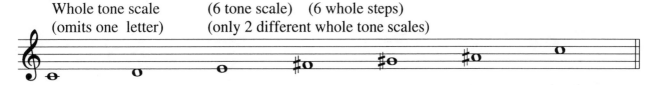

Diminished scale (w,1/2 start)

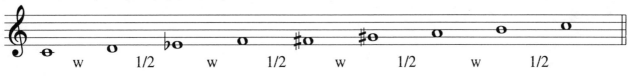

w   1/2   w   1/2   w   1/2   w   1/2

(1/2 - w start)

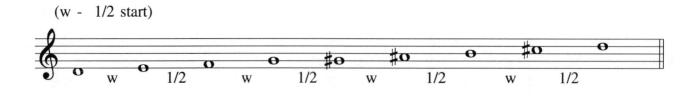

(w - 1/2 start)

Note: There are only 3 diminished Scales. Practice different starting and ending notes for all symmetrical scales and also occasionally sing the notes while playing.

The chromatic scale maybe used with any chord type and with any combination of alterations. Naturally, some scale tones will always be dissonant to the harmony and have a strong tendency to resolve. This resolution will probably be either up or down by a 1/2 step to the nearest chord tone.

Chromatic motion can create excitement if used sparingly. However, short chromatic groups of notes can generate melodic energy and certainly should not be avoided.

Because of its nature, the chromatic scale contains all of the conventional triads and seventh chords in all keys. It would be tedious and unnecessary to list them all.

Example:
    Augmented scale (+2 = minor 3rd)

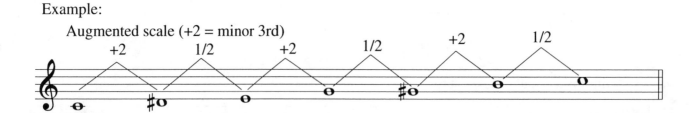

Examples

Symmetrical altered scales are often used to create ascending or descending melodic patterns which move through the scales in a logical progression. The following examples demonstrate patterns created by each scale form.

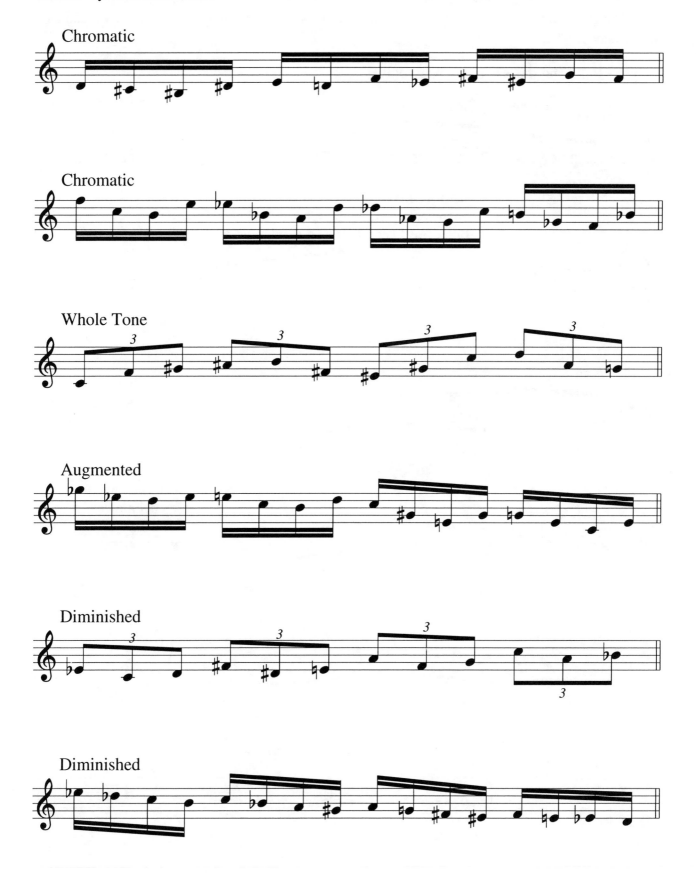

Root to Root Modes

The Major Scale is also known as the Ionian Scale. We usually play a major scale from its root to root. Using naturals and starting on a different note, the scale takes on a different quality... and each has a name to identify it.

Play the following modes. (white keys only)

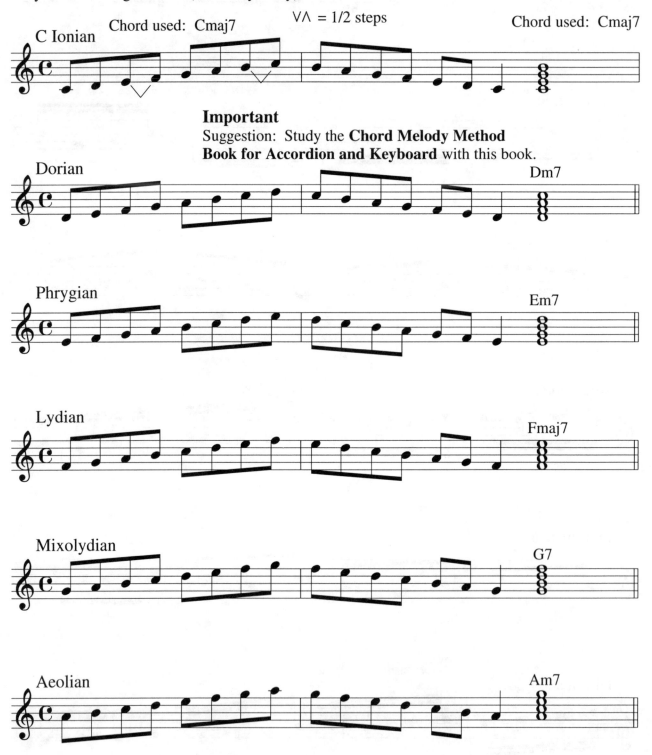

Important
Suggestion: Study the **Chord Melody Method Book for Accordion and Keyboard** with this book.

30

Locrian   Bm7-5

Though it is easy to find modes on the white keys, unfortunately they do not always occur in that key.

To use the modes effectively in composition or improvisation; it is essential to understand which tones (if any) are dissonant and need to resolve. The *odd - numbered scale tones of each mode are chord tones of its corresponding 7th chord and are generally no problem. Dissonant tones, however, require special handling (resolve) as the examples shown below.
Practice all modes in all keys and occasionally sing while playing. (All are written out for convenience)

∨∧ = 1/2 steps

C Ionian   Chord used: Cmaj7

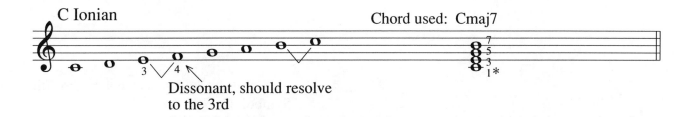

Dissonant, should resolve
to the 3rd

C Dorian   Cm7

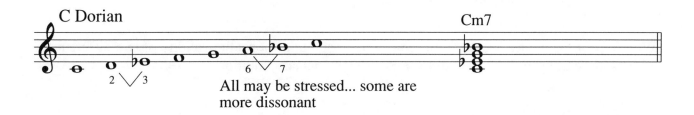

All may be stressed... some are
more dissonant

C Phrygian   Cm7

Dissonant
resolve downward 1/2 step

C Lydian   Cmaj7

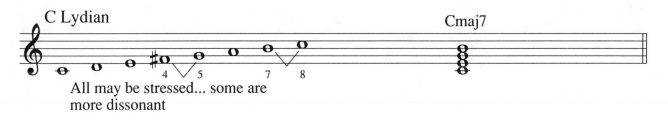

All may be stressed... some are
more dissonant

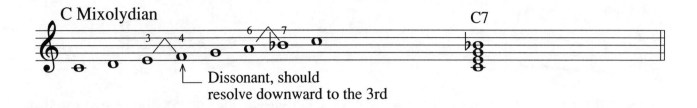

C Mixolydian   C7

Dissonant, should
resolve downward to the 3rd

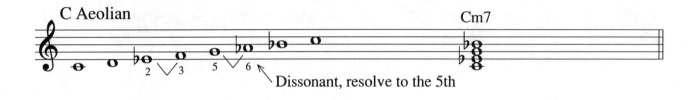

C Aeolian   Cm7

Dissonant, resolve to the 5th

(also known as the half dim. 7th)

Symbol: Cm7-5   or: C⌀

C Locrian

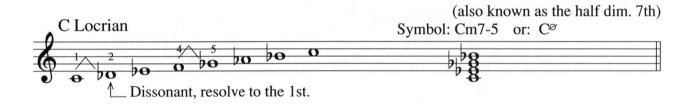

Dissonant, resolve to the 1st.

With four of the modes, we begin to see a comparison that shows the validity of two different traditions; the european classical tradition and the american jazz tradition.

Examples:

Cmaj7   C Ionian (Classical tradition)

Cmaj7   C Lydian (Jazz tradition) (Note the raised 4th)

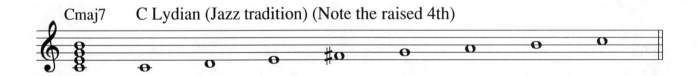

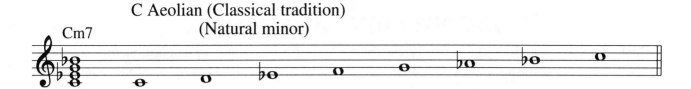

C Aeolian (Classical tradition)
(Natural minor)

C Dorian (Jazz tradition)

The important point to remember is that both traditions of music have validity and are of importance to the jazz musician. Even though some scales are not considered jazz scales as such; they very often serve certain musical situations as the most appropriate sounds to/for the flow of the composition.

Melodic Minor Scales

There are three minor scales; natural, harmonic and melodic as studied and practiced earlier. **The ascending melodic minor is the main focus for the jazz musician.** The descending form of the scale is generally disregarded and not used.

The ascending melodic minor is constructed by raising the 6th and 7th scale degrees of a natural minor scale one 1/2 step. **The unique quality of this scale is probably due to the fact that the first half of it is minor and the second half is major.**

In fact, another easy way to construct the ascending melodic minor scale is to simply lower the 3rd scale degree of a major scale one 1/2 step. (Momentarily disregard the key signature)

Examples: C Melodic Minor

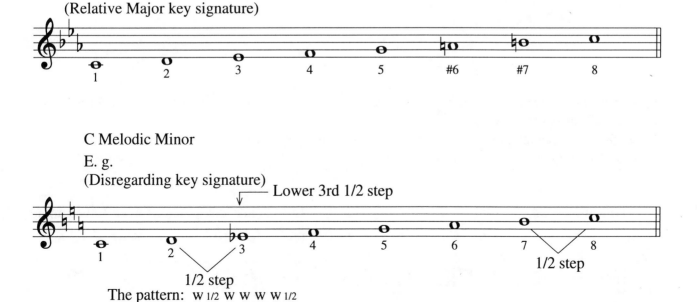

(Relative Major key signature)

C Melodic Minor

E. g.
(Disregarding key signature)
Lower 3rd 1/2 step

The pattern: w 1/2 w w w w 1/2

33

Pentatonic and Blues Scales

Most of us are familiar playing only the black keys on the piano or accordion; not everyone realizes that they form a pure pentatonic scale. A pentatonic scale is simply a five (penta-) tone scale. Generally the five tones within the octave forms a pentatonic scale; certain structures are most commonly used. The major pentatonic scale is one of the most common scales in music. You can easily learn to create melodies (improvisation) without being bound to chord changes. Hit songs that use the major pentatonic scale include: *My Girl, The Way You Do the Things You Do, I Saw the Light* and many more.

Example:

Gb Major Scale

Gb Major Pentatonic (Only Black Keys)

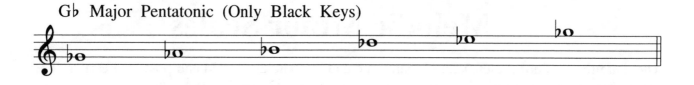

C Major Pentatonic

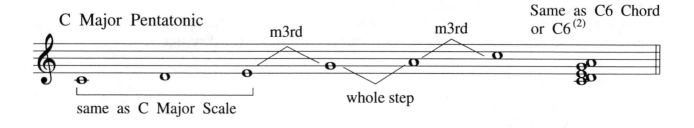

Here is a prime example of why it is so important to study the **Chord Melody Method Book** together with this scale book.

The author uses pentatonic scales primarily with a major 6th chord in mind in addition to the first 3 notes of its major scale. See above

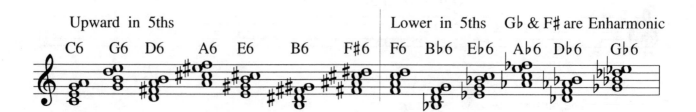

Play the following pentatonic scales using major 6th chords.

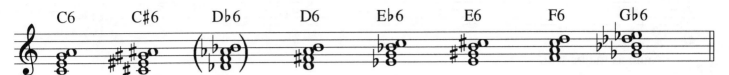

Minor Pentatonic

Examples:

Eb natural minor scale (relative to Gb major)

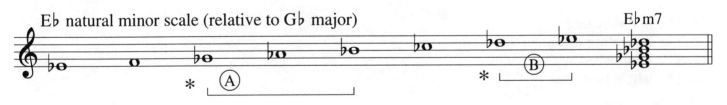

Eb minor pentatonic

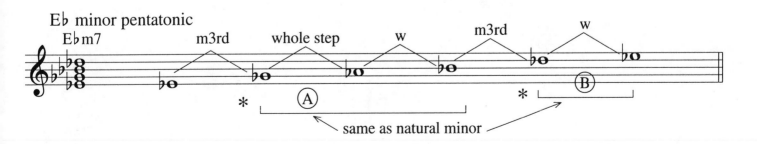

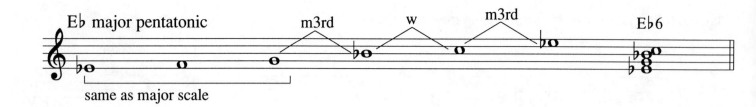

Eb major pentatonic — same as major scale — m3rd — w — m3rd — Eb6

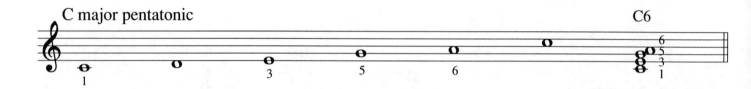

C major pentatonic — 1 — 3 — 5 — 6 — C6 — 6 5 3 1

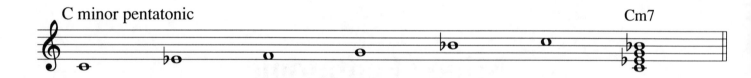

C minor pentatonic — Cm7

Even though we study and practice modal theory, the author is a firm believer in utilizing vertical chord tones horizontally with modal neighbor notes. The parallel study; **"The Chord Melody Method Book"** is extremely important for chord memorization and application. Remember, the four primary scales to use with all chords are:

1. The major scale
2. The ascending melodic minor
3. The diminished scale
4. The whole tone scale

Blues Scales

The two most commonly used blues scales are what might be called modified pentatonics; (altered) that is, pentatonic scales with the addition of a 6th scale tone. Both scales include the traditional "Blue note," the lowered 3rd of the key; Example 2 adds the lowered 5th. Notice in the following examples that the first scale is a C major pentatonic with E♭ added and the second scale is a C minor pentatonic with G♭ (♭5) (F♯)

C Blues Scales

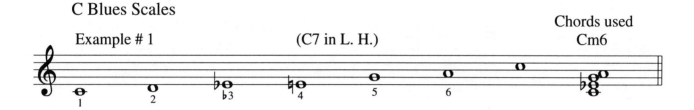

Both of these scales can be used with dominant 7th chords.

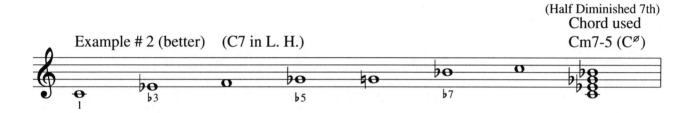

Synthetic Pentatonics

At the beginning of our pentatonic discussion the black notes of the piano were described as a "pure" pentatonic scale. However, neither the major or the minor pentatonic structure is applicable to certain chord types or altered situations. In such cases, either the major or minor form may be adjusted slightly to accomodate the proper chord.

(Synthetic cont'd)

Altered C major pentatonic   Cmaj7+5

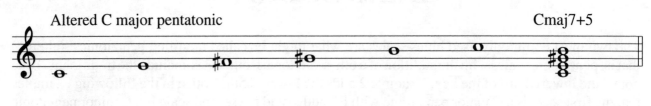

Altered C minor pentatonic ♭3   Cm6

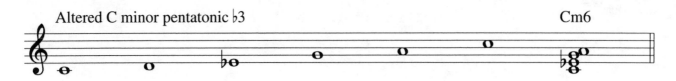

Altered C minor pentatonic ♭3   Cm6

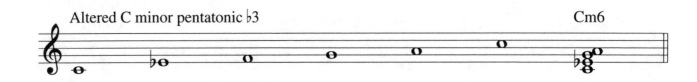

Altered C minor pentatonic ♭5   Cm7-5

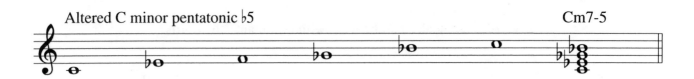

Of course, the possibilities for the creation of synthetic pentatonic scales are many.

Extra staves for teacher notes

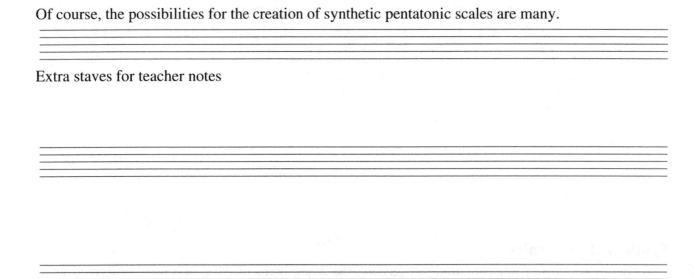

MODES: Key of G (remember to occasionally sing along)

Ionian

Dorian

Phrygian
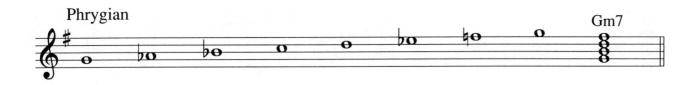

Lydian

Mixolydian
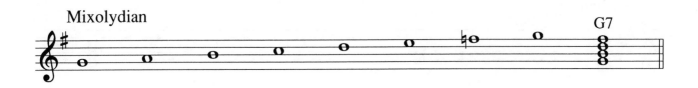

Aeolian
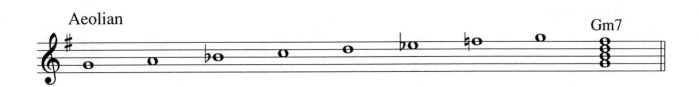

Locrian Gm7-5

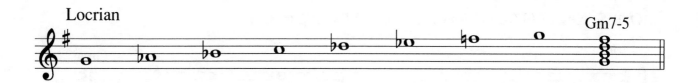

Key of D

Ionian Dmaj7

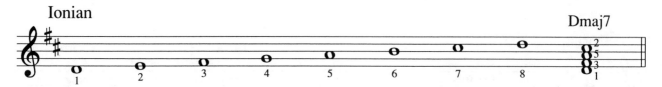

Dorian Dm7

Phrygian Dm7

Lydian Dmaj7

Mixolydian D7

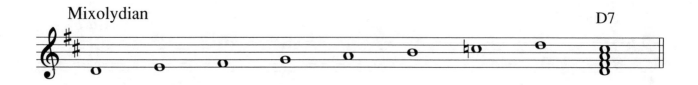

Aeolian   Dm7

Locrian   Dm7-5

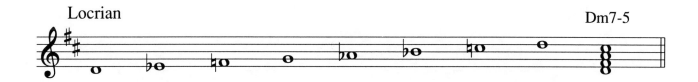

Key of A

Ionian   Amaj7

Dorian   Am7

Phrygian   Am7

Lydian   Amaj7

Mixolydian

A7

Aeolian

Am7

Locrian

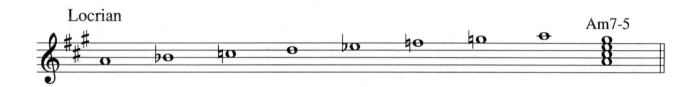

Am7-5

Key of E

Ionian

Emaj7

Dorian

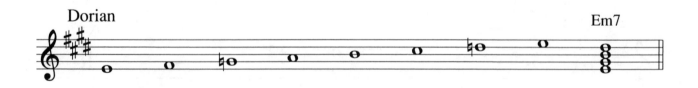

Em7

Phrygian

Em7

Lydian Emaj7

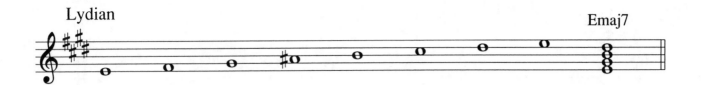

Mixolydian E7

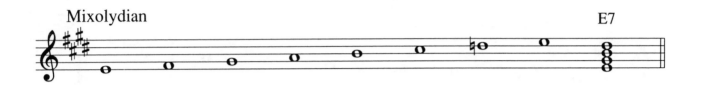

Aeolian Em7

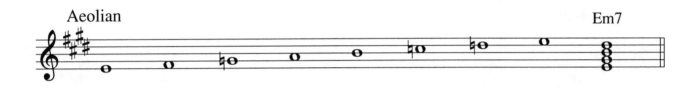

Locrian Em7-5

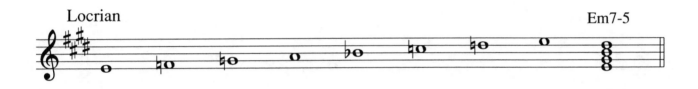

Key of B

Ionian Bmaj7

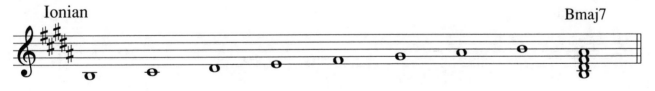

Dorian Bm7

Phrygian   **Bm7**

Lydian   **Bmaj7**

Mixolydian   **B7**

Aeolian   **Bm7**

Locrian   **Bm7-5**

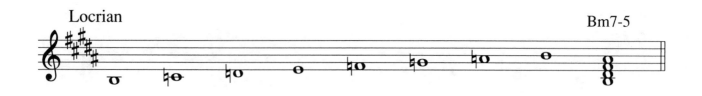

Key of F#

Ionian   **F#maj7**

Dorian   F#m7

Phrygian   F#m7

Lydian   F#maj7

Mixolydian   F#7

Aeolian   F#m7

Locrian   F#m7-5

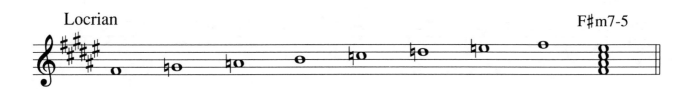

Key of F

Ionian  Fmaj7

Dorian  Fm7

Phrygian  Fm7

Lydian  Fmaj7

Mixolydian  F7

Aeolian  Fm7

Locrian   Fm7-5

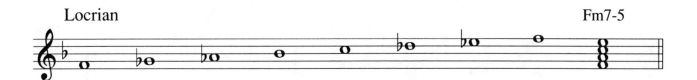

Key of B♭

Ionian   B♭maj7

Dorian   B♭m7

Phrygian   B♭m7

Lydian   B♭maj7

Mixolydian   B♭7

Aeolian   **B♭maj**

Locrian   **B♭m7-5**

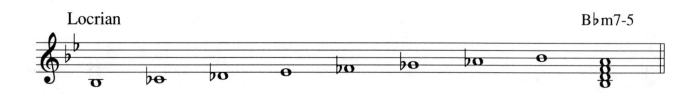

Key of E♭

Ionian   **E♭maj7**

Dorian   **E♭m7**

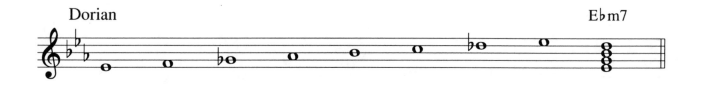

Phrygian   **E♭m7**

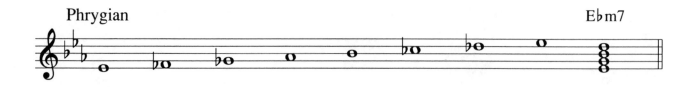

Lydian   **E♭maj7**

Mixolydian — E♭7

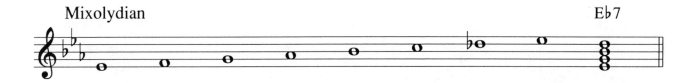

Aeolian — E♭m7

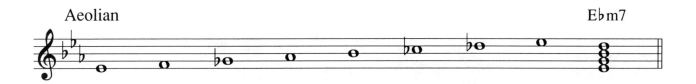

Locrian — E♭m7-5

Key of A♭

Ionian — A♭maj7

Dorian — A♭m7

Phrygian — A♭m7

49

Lydian   A♭maj7

Mixolydian   A♭7

Aeolian   A♭m7

Locrian   A♭m7-5

Key of D♭

Ionian   D♭maj7

Dorian   D♭m7

Phrygian

D♭m7

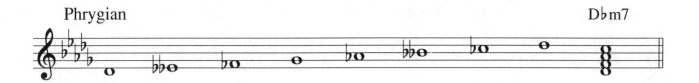

Lydian

D♭maj7

Mixolydian

D♭7

Aeolian

D♭m7

Locrian

D♭m7-5

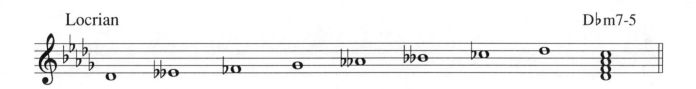

Key of G♭

Ionian

G♭maj7

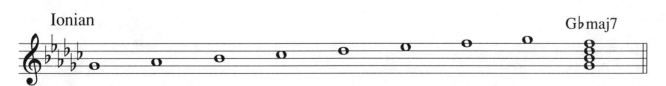

Dorian   G♭m7

Phrygian   G♭m7

Lydian   B♭maj7

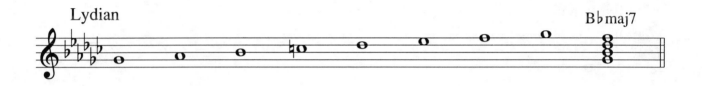

Mixolydian   G♭7

Aeolian   G♭m7

Locrian   G♭m7-5

Brazeal

Jazz Samba
Dedicated to Art Van Damme
... The use of jazz scales and chords

Any Tempo

Gary Dahl
2/2001

* Enharmonic for Bass Keyboard

54

* Examples of Jazz Scales and Chords from Melbay's Jazz Accordion Solos by Gary Dahl MB96309BCD (with CD)

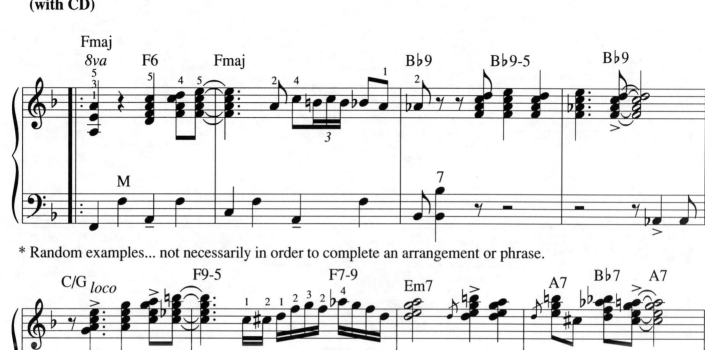

* Random examples... not necessarily in order to complete an arrangement or phrase.

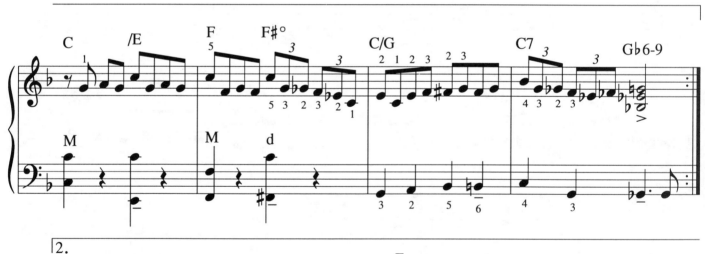

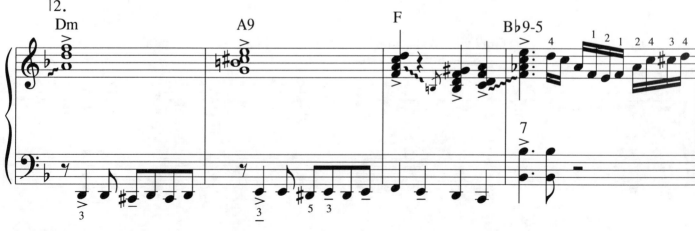

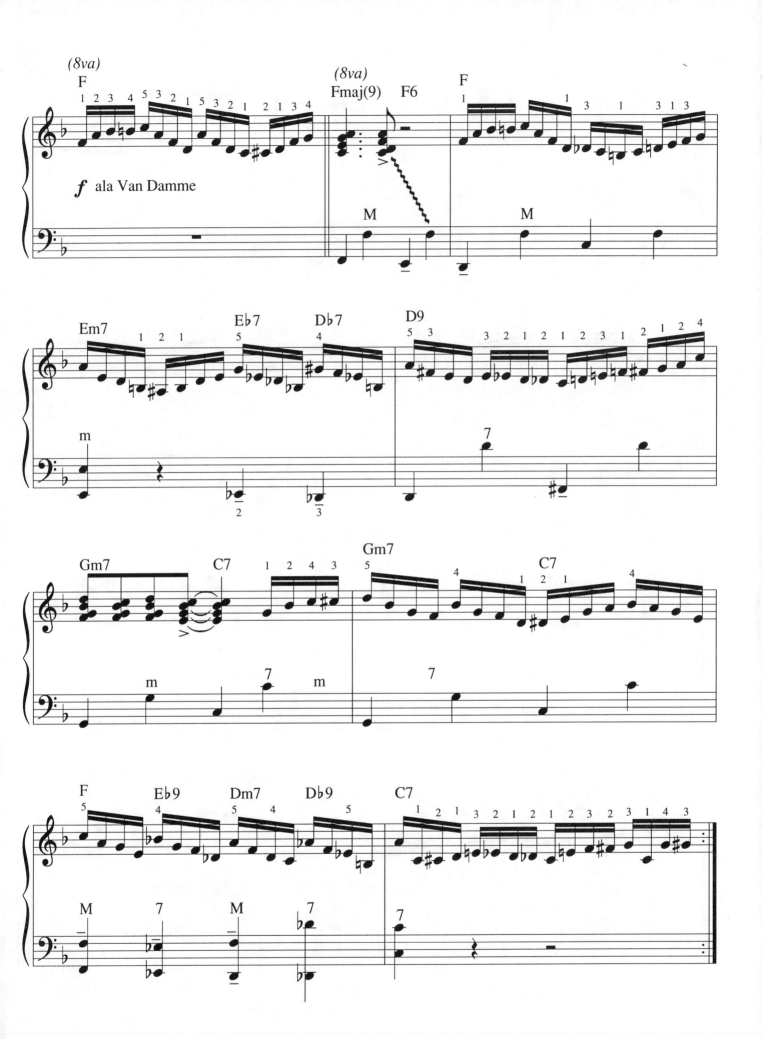

60

ala Van Damme

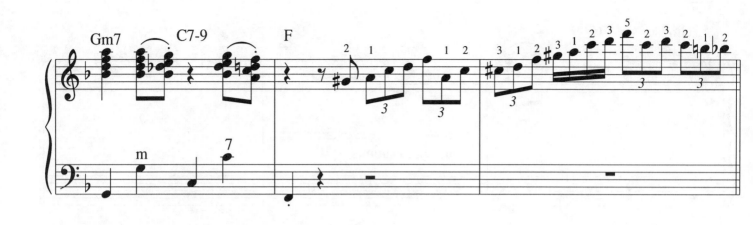

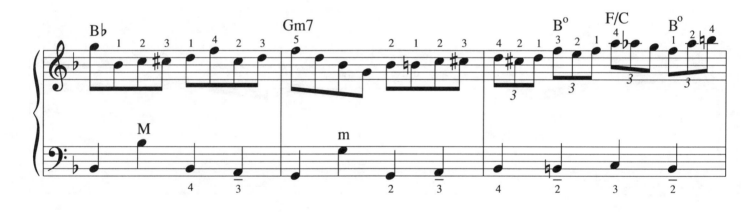

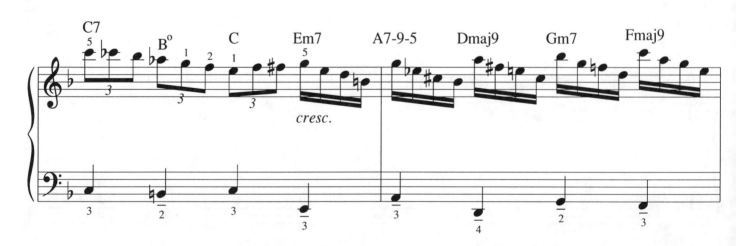

ala Van Damme

cresc.

Rockin' The Blues

Rock/Blues Training
Groove Tempo - Medium

Gary Dahl

Watch Your Bach

Jazz Accordion Solo

Dedicated to Joe Spano

Gary Dahl

75

Note: Additional dynamics and styling at the discretion of the accordionist.